DS VERNON

Peripheral

To those who are gone
And those they left behind

Foreword

Somebody once mentioned to me in a conversation long enough ago so that I can't recall when exactly I had it or with whom that it was entirely likely that the world's smartest, or most gifted, or creatively talented individuals never once set about working or doing anything within those areas they were so talented.

The implication was simple to arrive upon - somewhere, and somewhen, there probably existed a woman who may have put Emily Dickinson's poetic achievements and expressions to shame given the right set of circumstances; or dwarfed Marie Curie's grasp of the physical sciences if given the opportunity; or whose presence and charisma could have made a singular figure like Golda Meir seem like a paper tiger were she from the right family and presented with the career path.

The thought experiment, be it one that speaks to the awesome potential of the human experience, is also a depressing one filled with 'what-ifs' and the sobering realization that we as a species do not do nearly enough to cultivate and encourage those among us that carry such potential to enrich our lives, push our knowledge of the world around us to its limits, or to lead us into that unknown every tomorrow holds for us.

*

I first met DS last November online through friends of friends and family, as a person described as having a great enthusiasm for writing as well as the genres of writing I'm most enthusiastic for – those being horror, science-fiction, and the like. I ended up reading a short submission of his, which in retrospect now feels like the prototype or precursor of the tale which you are about to read. It was written in a voice that was crying out to be heard and shared with the world, a voice that seemed to say (at least to me) that "not all is well, even in the worlds that are assumed to shine the brightest – here, let me show you…"

In that sense, DS represented to me a writer with such a unique and refreshing approach to the craft that to allow that voice to go unheard would be tantamount to what I mentioned in the section previous. Maybe not on the order of an Emily Dickinson, but the world does not ask for another Dickinson.

Or Whitman, or even a poet as either.

A craftsman within the field of fiction, and one that stands within society as an individual who is all of these things:

A wonderful father.

A loving and devoted husband.

A hardworking and dedicated individual within his chosen career.

And a dear friend.

But despite all of these things that we may strive for, DS possesses the depth of character and moreover, the skills of both expression and…perception…to see those things that lurk within the shadows that haunt in the best of us.

I am very proud, and humbled to present to you DS Vernon's

first solo publication because:

He'd like most of all, to tell you about those things that watch
and wait and follow us – in our peripheral...

• wp Quigley
September 2023

ONE

"We therefore commit this body to the ground, earth to earth, ashes to ashes, dust to dust; in sure and certain hope of the Resurrection to eternal life." The pastor turned and placed a hand on Theresa Dolen's casket and bowed his head. While he uttered a few silent words of prayer, the crisp April breeze pulled his gray hair out of its neatly combed position. He turned back to the gathered crowd.

"The Dolens would like to invite everybody to join them at the reception hall at Beaumont Fields for lunch directly following these services. Thank you everyone for coming and paying your respects today. Go in peace to love and serve the Lord. The ceremony is now concluded."

As the pastor finished, an assistant from his church played "Ave Maria" through a small gray stereo with a built in CD player that looked displaced from a late 90s Walmart, likely purchased with some leftover money from the collection baskets. Most of the music was carried away in the wind. Up close, the low power speakers struggled to handle the music at its current volume and periodic distortion reverberated through the otherwise beautiful song.

Raymond Dolen, sat in one of the few folding chairs that

1

made something of a front row for the grave-site services for his wife. He wasn't actively sobbing at this point, only staring, tears occasionally slipping out; no longer an active rain, but a forgotten item left in the passing storm, trying to drip itself dry while the world moves on.

And the world already was beginning to move on, Raymond could feel. As soon as the pastor started to thank them, people started shuffling, making sure they had their bags and coats and whatever else, preparing to move to their cars and away from this place of death and sadness. Taking their first steps in moving on. Many of them would have fully moved past their grief by the end of the week, or the end of the day. Some would move on with life by the time lunch was served.

But he was here, unmoving, so mired in his grief, Raymond thought he might never move from this seat.

His thoughts were cast back to time when he was young and his dad had brought him and his brother and his Aunt Tina out on his motor boat while on a vacation in Maine. Raymond clung to an inner tube tied by a long length of rope to the back of the boat. He had been laughing and having fun but then the rope frayed and simply just let go. He was floating in the middle of the lake as the boat sped away, leaving him behind. Isolated, alone, adrift, clinging to that tube and sure that if his grip loosened he would slip into the dark waters of the lake and he would never see his father, brother, or Aunt Tina again.

Amanda leaned in and laid her head on his shoulder. The recognizable smell of the color-safe shampoo that she'd been using since she started dying her hair in high school (cruelty-free, sulfate-free, and vaguely fruit scented) wafted up to him as she did. Raymond found the smell familiar and calming in this moment. He leaned his head on hers and tried to focus on that feeling while it lasted.

"Dad, you did such a good job with everything. Mom... she would have loved it." She sniffed hard, mostly out of tears, and tucked some rogue wisps of her now-auburn-hair behind her ear.

Raymond sighed deeply, "Thank you, Mandy."

The plot he and Amanda had picked out was a nice one. It was way in the back of the cemetery. The last plot in this particular section to be used. It was under a tree so it would have nice shade for visitors. The seclusion, at least, was peaceful.

They sat like that a while longer while guests filtered by. Some took flowers from the bouquets arranged on the casket to save in water, or press and keep forever in a beautiful but grim sentimentality. Raymond supposed they were the same in the end. He'd seen this done before at other memorial services, but for some reason this particular behavior stood out as especially morbid to Raymond. At least it seemed that way here at his Theresa's memorial. But there were certain tasks and traditions everybody expected, even Theresa, so he made good.

Something in the corner of his eye caught Raymond's attention. It fluttered and danced in the way only something on the edge of one's vision can, bringing with it only the shadow and hint of a color; blue. Raymond turned to look at whatever it was. He saw, far in the distance of the cemetery, a groundskeeper walking the edge of the fence with a weed whacker. Raymond could see that he wore some kind of ear protection but at this distance the tool sounded like a small insect flying by his ear. The man wore greens and browns. The weed wacker was orange.

Raymond furrowed his brow. The sky was a perfect overcast, a pale cement dome, empty and uncaring. He could have sworn it was something blue catching his attention but -

Amanda nudged him. "Everybody's gone. We need to get to Beaumont."

The two stood up. They looked at the casket for another minute and began walking to their limousine, the only vehicle left on the graveyard road.. By the time they got to the car, the driver had already opened their respective doors. Raymond noted that this man, whose sole job was to drive them here and there in this gaudy automobile, was the only person who hadn't moved on without them. He and Mandy climbed in, Raymond walking around to the far side, both of them feeling awkward. The last time either of them had been in a limo was fifteen years ago, when Theresa's mother – Mandy's grandmother - had passed. For what other occasion does one rent limos, other than funerals...and proms?

The doors closed behind them. One. Two.

The world around them was muffled then. They sat, removed from even each other, closed off and quiet. The calm at the end of a storm. The calm before the beginning of another.

This silence, which felt like hours to Raymond and Amanda but was no more than mere moments, was only broken by the sounds the driver made as he set about his next task. The gravel crunching under his feet. The door opening and closing. The limo starting. The sounds the small rocks made as they came out from under the tires.

TWO

When Theresa died, succumbing at last to her illness, the day that followed was as horrible for Raymond as it was surreal. He had left the hospital the previous evening, the nurses telling him to go get some rest and come back in the morning. Raymond had acquiesced, only to get "The Call" a few hours later.

As painful as receiving that call was, it paled in comparison to having to then call Amanda. Paled compared to saying out loud for the first time that Theresa had died.

He had gone back to the hospital so late at night after the nurse had called to say she had died. He sat there with Amanda and Theresa's body in that suddenly cold and unfeeling hospital room. No life there, only quiet machines that no longer hummed or beeped; metal and plastic statues looming over this sterilized corpse-garden.

They had to take down all the get well cards, pack up all the flowers, and remove all other personal effects. Packing up the photographs was the worst. Looking at all the smiling faces that once brought some cheer to Theresa, now relegated to far gone memories. Antiques. Relics. What was, not what is. Never what is.

By the time all this was done and they drove back home from the city, it was nearly four in the morning. Raymond, of course, did not fall gently to sleep. He tossed and turned reliving the days events, from when he'd last seen Theresa alive all the way through cleaning up her hospital room just hours ago. He didn't know when it was that exhaustion took him, but it was sometime after the full dark of night started to give way to the first hints of dawn.

Because of this, Raymond slept late. Raymond was a person that typically slept-in on the weekend to a time of eight, maybe eight-thirty. So when his eyes peeled back and his first sight was his bedside clock showing the time to be eleven thirty-eight, it was disorienting.

11:38. The red glowing numbers flushed in the blue of late morning light.

He had awoken the same way he had for the last few months of his life. Everything felt as it had. But Theresa, of course, was not in the bed with him. She was at the hospital and he would soon get ready to go visit her.

No. He wouldn't be doing that at all.

This realization hit him just as hard as it did when the nurse called the night before. Its impact just as profound. For those blessed hours of sleep and more importantly the few sweet seconds after sleep, Theresa was still alive, in the hospital sure, but still alive to him. And then the cruelty of fully waking up pulled away that habitual thought and reality came back, sandblasting away the rusted hope and happiness.

When he was finally able to calm himself and get out of bed, everything was just... wrong. It was too late in the day to be getting up. He had his first coffee of the day but it was getting to be lunch time. The morning had disappeared and he was thrust

6

forward in the day just as surely as he was thrust forward in life without Theresa. He drank his coffee with a turkey sandwich for lunch. Nothing fit.

He looked out the side window in his kitchen and off towards the street. The cars went by as they always did. People going about their business as they always did. Everything was different but nobody seemed to know or care. Tears welled in his eyes again.

Raymond breathed in deeply, his breath shaking the whole way in. He exhaled, steadier now. He blinked a long slow blink and turned from the window and moved to the living room to sit on the couch.

He had left his cell phone there. Looking at the home screen, he saw that he had missed eleven calls, nearly half from Amanda. The others were from various family members. He couldn't bring himself to call anybody just yet, but he did listen to the three voicemails that people had actually bothered to leave. Perhaps "sorry about your dead wife" was too awkward for some people to record. None of those voicemails were from Amanda. She never left voicemails. She sent follow up texts instead.

Raymond checked his messages. Eight texts from Amanda, left in increasing degrees of inquiry about his current state. "Are you awake yet?", "Call me when you can.", and finally, "I'll just come over around 1. If you're not awake, I have my key."

"K hun" was all he could muster in a return text.

True to her word, Amanda was at the house just after one o'clock. She let herself in and silently closed the door, not sure if her father had sent his eventual reply text from bed. But she turned the corner to the living room to find her father sitting on the couch in the dark, his cell phone carelessly tossed onto the coffee table in front of him.

Amanda glanced around and noticed that he hadn't opened any of the shades in the house apart from the one by the driveway that looked out toward the street. She started moving about the house opening all of them.

"Hi Dad," she called as she began her task.

"Hey kid," came back softly.

He made no move to get up and help, nor did he try and stop her. He was indifferent to the situation in a way that Amanda was unused to seeing. It made her uncomfortable, but she pushed through it, needing to do something at all to feel useful.

"Dad, do you need lunch or anything?" she asked, leaning in from the kitchen.

"No, hun. Already ate."

She glanced around the kitchen. There were no dishes in the sink. The bread was unwrapped and sitting near an empty deli bag on the counter. She put together pretty quickly that he had eaten over the sink.

Amanda came over to Raymond and sat with him, he on the couch, she on the nearby love seat. They sat in silence for a while. Eventually, Amanda opted for turning on the TV.

The channel that came on was playing an old episode of the Golden Girls. Bea Arthur stood over Betty White, with Arthur's characteristic disapproving look on her face. White was sitting and playing the piano. They started singing a song about Miami, interrupted periodically by their usual bickering. Amanda turned to her father with a forced smile on her face, clearly hoping that he would be amused by their on-screen banter.

But Raymond burst into tears.

The grief had come back at full force and all at once. Simply hearing the word Miami, had shattered any semblance of stability he thought he had. He cried freely.

Amanda moved next to him and held him.

"Dad... what?"

"Miami," he managed to squeeze out.

Amanda hugged him closer, her own eyes welling up for him.

THREE

The function room at Beaumont Fields was large and light, thanks to one whole wall being made up of windows that extended from roughly knee-height all the way to the ceilings. The half of the room closest to the windows was filled with arranged tables and chairs. The side further away contained a bar and a buffet station. Everything seemed to be inoffensive shades of tans and grays.

When they finally got there, Raymond realized he and Amanda had been the last to arrive. Everybody turned and looked as they walked in but they all seemed to simultaneously try and hide it and casually go back to their conversations. Except for Aunt Tina, who did the double take, but took it upon herself to walk over. The emissary of everybody else, Raymond supposed.

"Rayyyymond. Amandaaaa…." She hugged them both at the same time.

Aunt Tina was Raymond's father's youngest sister. So much younger than his father was Tina that she was almost an older sister to Raymond, both in age and relationship. Although she had always acted like a wizened old protector, even when they were young.

For the longest time Aunt Tina had her short read hair cut to above her shoulders. She always had on a set of circular glasses with rims thicker than were in fashion. Raymond thought she was modeling herself off Molly Ringwald in Pretty in Pink. She seemed to have made that choice back in the late 80s and just stuck with it ever since.

"Here, please. Come with me." Aunt Tina said, "We have a seat for you. They said they would start bringing the buffet things out after you'd arrived."

She lead them over to a seat with other members of the family. Raymond was so tired at this point from the work of funeral arrangements and the general lack of sleep that he just allowed himself to be moved around and sat down. After they were situated, Aunt Tina went off to tell the manager that Raymond had arrived and the buffet could begin. The family members at the round table he happened to have been sat at, nodded and gave their sad smiles. They were at the funeral earlier, and wake before that. What more is to be said right now?

Raymond did his best to participate in the conversations at hand. But it was difficult. Through his exhaustion and distraction he was having trouble mustering up any care for what was being said.

It was just a few minutes after the third or fourth prodding from Aunt Tina that he should go eat, that he started seeing something - and not just the hint of a color - in his peripheral vision.

FOUR

I n days that immediately followed Theresa's death, Raymond continued to have a difficult time functioning in even the most rudimentary senses. He didn't sleep for more than four hours in a given day. Sometimes those hours occured all at once. More often however, was that half of that time happened somewhere in the night where they should have occurred, while the rest came dead in the midst of the rest of the world's waking hours. He was in a fog, the misery of his situation intermingled with an extreme yet vague exhaustion. It left numb even to his own existence.

Theresa's remains had been brought to McNeil Funeral Home from the hospital - one of three in the town in which they'd lived. This much Raymond had managed to decide on his own, and for those days that came thereafter he had done nothing else that required his attention. McNeil would end up calling two or three times a day for most of the following week, but Raymond had ignored the calls. Raymond ignored every call that came, the numbers appearing and then disappearing on his cell phone, the message indicator reaching double digits without his so much as even acknowledging his voicemail even existed.

It wasn't until the morning Amanda had come by to check

on him that things finally began to move forward. She had been frightened to death as she made her the drive over to her parents' home that something had also happened to her father when he stopped answering her calls and texts. She was frantic when she came through the front door. Instead, she merely found him in a far more disassociated state – one infinitely worse than the one she'd found him in the day after her mother had passed. It seemed to break the second he laid eyes upon her.

That afternoon, the phone calls, including those from Mc-Neil's were answered and acknowledged. Mandy's arrival had cleared the fog, even if it was temporary and as a result of her physical presence.

Many people in the family – both from Theresa's side as well as Raymond's - tried to help where they could. Most of this came by way of prepared meals they had brought to the house. Raymond was thankful he didn't have to cook, but he was nowhere near as hungry as everybody seemed to think he was. So much of it ended up frozen and stuck the icebox. Theresa had been the cook, so at least it would be a while before he had to teach himself.

Regardless of the good intentions of family the friends that turned up, - even the presence of his daughter - Raymond had to handle the details of Theresa's wake, funeral, will, and everything else that came with the loss of a spouse mostly alone.

The sheer amount of things he was then responsible for deciding and completing seemed insurmountable, daunting, and incredibly frustrating in its near endlessness.

He had to select a funeral "package" that included certain wake and funeral amenities, a casket, and a cemetery.

He had to write an obituary, which thankfully, Amanda had

been incredibly helpful with penning. He had sat down to do this, and before he set a single word to the page he'd yelled to an empty room:

"How the hell are you supposed to sum my wife's life up in a couple of words?!" Amanda had heard him yell and came in and took the laptop away from him, saying that she would give it a try. In truth, the funeral home had offered something of a template to start with and she had made the changes and expansions, though she did so eloquently and lovingly.

He had to pick which bouquets of flowers would be on display in the funeral home and at her grave.

He had to pick a goddamn dress for Theresa, then and decide if she should be wearing jewelry.

He had to find pictures and photos of Theresa, to put up around McNeil's for the wake. Mandy had a few, but mostly they came from scrapbooks and social media posts he pored through.

He had to figure out what church was going to deliver the funeral mass.

He had to give the pastor some shit to say (*he didn't know Theresa - none of those pastors or priests ever knew anyone, they just pretended to and used notes they'd been given*).

He had to figure out who would get up to talk about her and her life (*among the people who actually did know her*).

And then, at last, find a place to go have a perfunctory meal after all was said and done. By the time that this task was all that was left for him to do, Raymond had regressed back into the state he had been in prior to Mandy's arrival. Unable to focus. Raymond's brother Martin finally stepped in and found Beaumont.

Martin had said to him:

"Look, Ray, I took care of the reception booking. Just tell everyone you made it, okay? People are going to be looking to you for strength when it comes to losing Theresa. If it comes out I had to do this for you, people will start talking. Okay?"

Raymond had been incredibly grateful for his brother…but in the back of his mind resentful as well. Why was booking a damn reception hall a sign of outward strength? And why is it that *he* had to be *strong* right now? He had been pushed so far past his limits for the last ten days, he would never have found a place half this nice – this much was true. But in the end, what difference did it really make?

His wife was gone. That was all that really mattered to Raymond in that moment.

FIVE

When he saw the thing in his peripheral vision he was reminded of sitting in his office at home with the window to his right, open to the fresh air and sounds of nature. Every so often a bird would fly by, close enough that he'd register the movement almost on instinct. But when he would turn, nothing was there – the bird well on its way to wherever and far removed from the visibility allowed by Raymond's window.

He knew the movement came from somewhere outside of the large windows of the function room, a blue fluttering, not unlike a bird just beyond the range of his direct vision. He spun in its direction to catch the full measure of the thing. But when he looked head on there was nothing to regard.

No flocks of birds perched on the edges of the nearby hills. The trees that were out there were too far away to really be to blame for what he felt like he was registering.

No groundskeepers were outside, mowing or raking this time, either. Just quiet, serene April countryside trying to come back to life underneath the overcast sky.

Raymond rubbed his eyes and excused himself from the conversation. He got up and went to the buffet, if only to placate Aunt Tina. He got what he could from the serving trays, trying to stick with food that wouldn't sit too heavy. Instead of taking his previous seat, he found an empty table right near the windows and sat down.

He watched the landscape and waited.

Nothing.

After some indeterminate amount of time, long enough certainly for his plate of food to cool well below being appetizing, Amanda came and sat next to him. She slid a drink to him.

"Hmm?" The noise of the sliding glass had snapped him out of his contemplations.

"Jameson and ginger."

"That's my drink. Thank you, Mandy."

The two sat in a strangely comfortable silence, watching the world outside and ignoring the rest of the gathering. Nobody seemed to mind that they'd taken up a position removed from the rest of the reception. It would have been too awkward for anyone to even approach them, anyway. They drank their drinks and bought each other refills.

Raymond occasionally rubbed his eyes, unable to shake all-too-frequently appearing collagen floaters drifting through and then past his vision.

Eventually, their rented time in the hall came to a close. Lots of hugs followed with lots of insistences that Raymond should "just call" if he needed anything.

Raymond thought about his previous inability to even call the funeral home on his own. He never said that out loud though. There were some nods and some thank yous and some milling about the parking lot – the kind you do when you know something is over and there is nothing more to be done, but there is an unease in its completion.

When we leave this place, its really over, thought Raymond

Aunt Tina's son Christopher offered to drive he and Amanda back to Raymond's house since they had been originally picked up there by the limo. They gratefully accepted, taking their respective seats in the back of his sedan. Aunt Tina rode along, as well in the front passenger seat.

"Ray, I hope you don't mind," Christopher said almost hesitantly, "but I can't drive without some music going. I'll keep it quiet though."

"Please, Christopher, you're giving us a ride in your car. Whatever you need, kid." Raymond replied.

Christopher played with his phone for a minute. "Should I Stay or Should I Go" began. Christopher backed out from his parking spot.

Aunt Tina then talked over Christopher's music for the entire ride. She was never one to be comfortable in silence, music not withstanding. Luckily, Christopher was able to keep the conversation, as it were, going with a series of well timed, uh-huh's and that's right's. Aunt Tina kept the other half up just fine.

Bless that boy, Raymond thought.

He loved his Aunt Tina dearly and she had been incredibly supportive, but he just did not have the capacity for banal conversation right now. He'd been cored and hollowed like an overripe apple and had nothing more to give.

Raymond stared out his window watching the suburbia roll past, barely even present in his own mind. That is until his eyes caught something in the distance. - Again.

Behind and between the houses he saw a figure. Too far away to see any details, but near enough to recognize it as a person. And enough to register a hint of blue. But what he saw didn't make sense.

As the car drove along and the colonials, split-level ranches, and occasional Victorian houses dragged infinitely past, this figure was static. Illuminated somehow, in the background behind all of them. It was like looking at an object behind the whirling blades of a fan. The figure blinked and fluttered as the fan-blade-houses went by.

Raymond stared, his face almost touching the side window. The music faded from his ears. Aunt Tina faded from his ears. His unblinking eyes the movie screen onto which this figure was being directly projected.

Abruptly, this all ended as Christopher quickly turned his car into Raymond's driveway, trying to beat the oncoming traffic. His quick application of the brake, quite literally shook Raymond from the state in which staring at this figure had left him.

"Dad...?" Amanda had seen him jump.

"I... no I'm fine, hun. I was just thinking about things. Not really paying attention."

Christopher was looking at them in the rear view. Aunt Tina had turned around, looking concerned. Raymond cleared his throat.

"Christoper, thank you. We appreciate the ride and everybody coming. Thank you."

"Yeah of course, Ray. You'll let us know if we can do anything to help out, right?"

"Yeah. We will. Thank you."

Amanda opened her door. "Thanks you guys."

SIX

From that same kitchen side window, the only one her father had bothered to raise the blinds on after her mother had died, Amanda watched Christopher and Aunt Tina pull away. When Christopher's car was out of sight, everything was left with a strange sense of finality. She continued staring at the street, long after. No cars went by.

At last, she turned and saw her father sitting at the counter. His suit jacket hung off the chair next to him. He had rolled up his sleeves and his tie had been loosened. She couldn't help but think that he looked 20 years older in that moment.

How much time is left before I'm an orphan? Amanda thought to herself.

The very notion of living without either of her parents made her physically recoil. She told her brain to shut the fuck up before it could continue on that train of thought, having only mild confidence that it actually would. Amanda's anxiety had been bad before her mother's passing, but had been on overdrive every day since.

It was three in the afternoon. Amanda couldn't help but feel like there was way too much day left for such a huge thing to have already happened and been done with. She also had no idea if her dad wanted her to stick around or wanted to rest by himself. She would ask, but she knew the kind of answer she was going to get – one that had no bearing on how her father truly felt about her presence either way.

"Dad. Should I… I mean, would you like some company for a while?"

"Mandy, you've already done enough. I don't mind if you go home. If you're not ready to go yet, stay. But if you're tired and need some time to yourself, go home and relax. Don't worry about your old man. I'll be fine."

She knew he was trying to be helpful and agreeable. And for a second there, she thought he meant what he said too. But what she really wanted to know was what *he* wanted. What he needed. After everything that had happened, with all the things he had to do and decide upon, he probably just didn't have the energy to even have an opinion. He probably didn't *actually* know what he wanted.

She decided on staying a bit for an afternoon coffee. They had both always liked sharing afternoon coffee and both had always derived a sense of peace from the communal experience. There was something inherently different about a coffee drank in the afternoon from the coffee of the morning. Despite the caffeine intake, there was a relaxing, centering aspect to it. It was something you have on a rocking chair on a front porch, watching cars bustle by while you stay still. She hoped to capture some of that feeling at that moment.

And for the next thirty minutes or so, it did bring a certain calmness. She noticed that her father seemed present, actually there with her in the here and now.. He wasn't in his thoughts, a million miles away. He commented on how well she made coffee and they talked about anything else but her mother. And

21

for now, that would have to do.

But eventually, this too would pass. Amanda would eventually have to go home. And what of her father then?

SEVEN

Amanda closed the door to her apartment and threw her keys on the kitchen table. She removed her coat and hung it over one chair and sat herself in another. Tilting her head back she exhaled deeply. After the events of the day and the last few weeks, she felt so...

Relieved.

A twinge of guilt crept up her throat at that realization, but she swallowed it down.

Why shouldn't she feel relieved? The difficulty of the funeral was over. The preparation for it had been hell, but that was over. Her mother's suffering was over. Her mother's grasp over her father was over.

Thats really not fair, now is it? She thought.

No, her father loved her mother with all his heart. Perhaps her mother had known it and embraced it and encouraged the doting behavior a bit, but she wasn't controlling over him.

Amanda knew that those thoughts came from her own suffering. They came from feeling left out and ignored as a child.

Raymond and Theresa. Oh and Amanda too.

She was the required piece to complete that little family. But once she was there, she was also the third wheel.

So yes. Relief. She was allowed to feel how she felt.

She got up from the table and took a glass from the dish rack. She opened the liquor cabinet. Pushing things around, she found the Jameson she'd picked up for visits from her father.

Not that he'd been around lately.

Understandably. Stop acting like a bitch, She squeezed her eyes shut and exhaled.

Grabbing a ginger ale from the fridge and ice from the door dispenser she assembled her father's signature drink. It wasn't her favorite drink, but it felt right in this moment.

She sipped the cocktail. As relieved as she was for herself and, to a lesser extent her mother, she she was worried for her Father.

He had not been the same since her mother had died. Even in the weeks leading up to her death he had been strong, unfaltering, and hopeful. But all of that withered and rotted like a forgotten jack-o-lantern in deep November, the second she died. She was going to have to be around for him as much as she could.

Even as she had that thought, the anxiety around that particular responsibility swelled.

She gulped down the rest of her drink and began assembling another.

She would do what she had to do to keep things together.

EIGHT

Raymond watched Amanda's car from his window, like she had watched Christopher's not an hour before, drive down the road and out of sight. The silence in behind in Amanda's departure was suddenly oppressive. Fom every corner, from every crack and crevice, it reached out for Raymond.

In any other time this silence might hang like a comfortable blanket around his shoulders, but now in the wake of his wife and all that followed, the it was like a plastic bag stretched tightly around his head, cutting off his oxygen and slowly killing him.

He turned the TV on. And turned it up.

"The White House released a statement on the matter saying-" Click.

No politics, he thought.

"Three people were found bur-" Click.

No news, he thought.

The sounds of a studio audience laughing filled the room. He put the remote down. He knew the show he landed on wasn't likely to make him laugh or even smile. He didn't really even like this one. Theresa had watched it often though. But more importantly, news, politics, anything remotely serious right now, he knew would probably just send him spiraling.

And so there he sat, staring into the void of the TV until the syndicated comedies from happier times switched over to serious programs of prime time. This shook him out of his trance. He looked around. Nothing had changed, since he had not changed it.

That's how things would be now.

Forever.

Raymond sighed and did what he could to not well up with tears again. He stood and picked up the discarded pieces of his suit from earlier. He shut the TV off since it was now a cop show talking about bloody cop-show things. He went upstairs and changed into some pajamas.

He turned the slightly smaller TV on in his bedroom and found the station that only played old comedies. It was one of the countless sitcoms from the 90s with the incompetent husband and the eye rolling wife. Perfect background noise that could be paid attention to or not.

The noise of it was all Raymond needed. Anything to stave off the suffocating silence from earlier.

He shut the light off and turned the ceiling fan on. Theresa was always hot at bedtime, so this fan was perpetually running at night. He couldn't bring himself to stop the tradition tonight.

Not yet.

Maybe not ever.

As soon as he laid down, exhaustion fell upon him like the falling walls of building being demolished. Pain, both physical and mental weighed heavier. The TV droned on. He stared into the whirring fan on the ceiling.

As he stared the sounds of the TV began to fluctuate and stretch as if slowed and sped up. Finally it began to hum, as if it had frozen a character in the middle of a word. The syllable stretched into forever.

But despite this strange auditory phenomenon, Raymond did not stop staring up at the ceiling. The fan spun. The pale blue light from the TV colored the ceiling above the fan and strobed and blinked as each blade cut by.

In the hum and flicker an image started to form.

The figure he saw from the car. Closer this time.

How did I forget about that? Raymond asked himself. But before he could formulate an answer, the figure began to move.

It turned around, and now it faced him. The details were still distant and unclear, dancing in the moving light. Whatever it was, it clearly now looked at him. It tilted its head to the side in contemplation. The figure reached a hand out toward him, the hand appearing to extend *through* the fan and stopping just inches from his face. Without thinking Raymond reached his hand back.

Studio audience laughter cut in at a deafening volume. Raymond blinked then snapped his head toward the TV. The hum was gone, the sitcom played on, now at full volume. He struggled with the remote and finally got it turned down.

Chest heaving, he laid back and looked into the fan again. But there was nothing. No figures reached from between the blades. It was as empty as he was.

NINE

Raymond was dreaming. He had this dream more than once since Theresa passed. He knew it was a dream even while he was having it. It was a less a dream, unlike any others he'd ever had in his life, and more a memory replayed exactly as he had experienced it when it had occurred.

It was the last time Raymond had seen Theresa alive. Although, at this point, alive was a technicality.

Raymond sat with Theresa in the hospital room. She was a wraith - everything human about her had long since been devoured...consumed. The cancer and the chemo had made damn sure of that. She had become so thin. He beautiful hair was gone. She still wore that bandanna she had for the last few months – the one with all the kittens, standing on their hind legs and holding their front paws up like an old-timey boxer, ready for some good ol' fashioned fisticuffs. It was cute while she still have a fighting chance. It was more sad and ironic now, like the kittens were going to try boxing bears.

She'd only been awake for a short time that day, maybe a half hour. She wasn't really able to speak anymore. But they had looked at each other lovingly, wordlessly, until she started to drift to sleep again. Before her eyes closed for the day, Raymond told her he loved her. A hint of a smile had crossed her face. As if that smile was the end of her strength reserves, her eyes fluttered and Theresa was asleep again.

He stayed with her that evening until he knew the worst of the traffic would have subsided in the city surrounding the hospital. Finally he gave Theresa one last squeeze of her hand with his own and a kiss on her forehead.

He walked to the doorway of the room, looking back on her in the bed. The machines around her quietly beeped, hummed, and exhaled. Cards and flowers decorated the window behind her. A whiteboard on the wall announced the name of the nurse on duty "Tiffany" followed by a smiley face. Raymond didn't know it right then, but Tiffany would be calling him in a few more hours.

"Goodbye, my love" he said aloud.

And then the dream ended.

TEN

"Nobody ever explains how much there is to do."

It had been three weeks since Theresa's funeral. Raymond still felt overwhelmed.

Although she had meant well, Aunt Tina had contributed to the persistence of this specific feeling just as often as she helped relieve it.

"Oh honey, no they don't. It is so much. I remember when..."

Aunt Tina's daily calls had tapered off to only three times a week from its previous seven. He couldn't decide if this was good or bad. Part of Raymond desperately wanted to vent about anything and everything. Another part of him was so very very tired of talking about all of it. He never knew which mood he was in until he picked up the phone and Aunt Tina had already launched into a conversation.

Today, Raymond found he had to stifle himself from snapping at her. He thought:

How the fuck would you know? You aren't even married. You spent your life living with Dad and Grandma. You've only had your own apartment for 15 years. You remember what? Seeing someone else in the family go through it?

Followed by:

Guess I'm in the "tired of talking about this" mood.

"Yeah, its a lot," he heard himself say out loud.

Despite, the occasional bubbling residual resentment and anger, he didn't actually feel compelled to get off the phone. Aunt Tina had already launched into her story about a friend who had lost her husband. He was sure he had heard this one before, but he didn't care. Listening to her tale was, in a way, like having company except he didn't have to get dressed or clean the house. And once she started off on a story, he didn't have to put much effort into the conversation, just drop in the occasional "uh-huh" or "yeah, I can see how that would be a lot". And Aunt Tina could talk to a wall.. Raymond didn't have the energy in him right now to be much more responsive than said wall, so it all worked out.

While Aunt Tina went along with her story, Raymond made himself another cup of coffee, absently adding sugar and finding the right shade of tan. He wandered over to the sliding glass door that looked out into his back yard.

He found himself standing here a lot. It was his contemplation spot, particularly while it was cold outside or while it was raining. Neither of those were true right now. It was sunny warm outside, relaxing and soothing in a way he normally loved. But still, he stopped at the door.

He used to sit on the back porch with Theresa on days like this. It was warm enough for him to enjoy and but not so warm that she would be hot. There were a handful perfect days in fall and spring where they were both comfortable in the air, nobody hot, nobody cold, that they could and frequently would spend the day outside, basking in the perfection of the weather.

"...The first time a light went out? With those high ceilings she had? Clara just did not know what to do..."

Aunt Tina was still going when Raymond spotted something at the treeline in his back yard. He knew what it was the second he caught sight of it.

The figure was back. And it was closer.

She was closer, he noted, for now it looked distinctly female. Still far enough away that the fine details remained impossible to properly discern, but now close enough that at least he could determine the gender of the figure.

He opened the slider and stepped onto the porch. The figure remained motionless.

He walked to the top of the small set of stairs. The figure tilted its head to the side again, seeming to consider him.

He walked down the 4 steps that brought him down to the stone patio. The figure turned and begin to walk into the woods, away from him.

"Hey wait!" he called after the phantom woman.

"Oh honey, what?!" Aunt Tina thought Raymond was calling to her, completely oblivious of what was befalling her nephew as they spoke. He still held the phone to the left side of his face. He seemed to have left his coffee somewhere else.

"What? Oh nothing Aunt Tina, it was just the mailman. I had something scheduled to be delivered today but I missed him. Go ahead."

"Oh, I'm sorry dear. Anyway - what was I saying? Oh right – her cat..."

Aunt Tina was on again. Raymond walked quickly toward the wood line.

The figure walked deeper into the woods, in a straight line so Raymond was able to watch where she went, , but strangely had reached a bizarre distance from his current position where it appeared as if she'd somehow drifted into his peripheral vision.

But then she paused. She paused there, halting her movements altogether. Raymond, however, kept after her. And when he drew close enough where her visage began to come into focus again, regaining its initial clarity, she turned to her left and disappeared behind a tree.

The tree she chose had a wide triangular base with curved bumps extending into the ground as if the roots started way too early and reached, grasping into the soil. Thick, gnarly bark, like pock marked battle-worn armor came next as the tree grew thin in its middle, and stretched high. Once the branches finally started, far over head, they reached like thin skeletal arms, leaves not growing until the very ends, think and heavy pulling back toward the ground. This tree, looked like it belonged in a swamp, not in a New England woodland surrounded by pines and oaks.

"And I swear if she didn't have that cat she would be lost!"

Losing sight of the figure, he began to panic, for reasons he couldn't quite explain. He broke into a sprint, one he kept up even once he'd traversed beyond the tree line. His bare feet were getting cut up by broken twigs and rocks that lay on the ground, but he didn't seem to notice. Finally, he made it to the tree.

The figure was gone.

All at once, the expanding balloon of panic that had grown in his chest burst. It released its contents into his chest and Raymond found it was filled not just with panic, but sadness, confusion, anger, and regret.

"Raymond, have you ever considered getting a pet?"

"Noooooo!" Raymond screamed., finally dropping the cell phone. It was primal. It came from the very heart of his being. He hadn't even heard Aunt Tina's question over his own wailing.

Instead, what he heard was sudden sharp and loud disorienting static coming from his cell phone. It sounded like an old snowy television in the days before cable or satellite or those scratchy spaces between radio stations. The sound grew until it was as loud as his scream had been.

The static flipped and fluttered as if an unseen hand began trying to tune an unseen radio far from any towers.

And at last, through the static came a voice:

"...that you...? ...Can't follow? Can...?"

Raymond scrambled for the phone, but the second he picked it up, the static ceased.

"My goodness, don't get a pet then, Raymond! It was just a suggestion!" Aunt Tina sounded flustered. She was responding to his scream – she clearly hadn't heard the static. No time had passed, at least from her perspective.

"I – No. Aunt Tina, I'm sorry. Its not the pet. Its a fine idea. I'll think about it I just – Its been a tough day. I'm sorry."

A beat passed.

"Its ok, honey. That was just – Do you think you are seeing somebody?"

Raymond started to sweat. How could she know?

"What did you say?"

"Have you thought about seeing somebody? Like a therapist or grief councilor?"

That's not what I heard. That's not what I heard. That's not what I heard.

"No, I don't think that's for me. People our age don't go to therapists. I'll be fine. I'm just sad, I'm not insane."

"Nobody said you're insane honey, listen -"

"Maybe we can talk about this later, Aunt Tina. I need to go. Love you." He ended the call and put the phone in his pocket.

Raymond wound his way back through the woods to his yard, only then noticing how cut up his bare feet were. Now he felt every stone and twig he stepped on and every once of dirt being pushed into the open wounds on his feet.

The walk back was slow and painful. Not just because of his feet. He thought about how he ran the woman, chased her, and was now returning to his home with nothing to show for it. Not a shred of any kind of evidence she'd ever been there.

He crossed back into his backyard proper and his house loomed ahead, seemingly larger and emptier. Everything inside, from the living room side window to the bedroom ceiling fan, from the televisions to the coffee cups from which only he would drink reminded him of what and who was lost. It was like living in a sepulcher.

And at that moment, he wasn't entirely sure who had been laid to rest within anymore, his wife Theresa…or the shattered remains of his life.

When he reached the bottom of the stairs to his deck, he found his discarded coffee cup. It had landed on its side in the overgrown weeds of the once decorative flower garden. He and Theresa had planted it together to accent the small porch. He picked up his once full cup.

He looked inside regardless, and dropped it back to the ground the second his mind registered what had taken the place of the coffee he'd fixed himself.

The cup was filled, almost to the brim with maggots, twisting and pulsating in and over and around each other, colored the same shade of tan he made his coffee minutes before.

ELEVEN

The next day Raymond went out into the woods. No cell phone and prattering Aunt Tina to distract him this time. He wandered on sore feet through the woods trying to follow the path he had taken then night before, chasing the woman in the woods.

He wanted to find the spot she'd disappeared. He wanted to find that tree.

He'd spent some time online trying to figure out exactly what kind of tree that was. He was sure he'd seen trees like it before, but certainly nowhere around here.

When he'd finally found his answer, it didn't bring him any comfort at all.

Taxodium distichum. Bald Cypress. Native to the Florida Everglades.

Raymond needed to see this tree again and see if the figure might show herself again.

Raymond entered a sudden clearing in the trees. He was sure this is where he'd followed the woman last night. He turned around confirming the relatively straight path back to his house. This had to be the spot. He even found the indent where he'd fallen to his knees to retrieve his cell phone as the static-scream tuned to words.

None of that mattered though. There was no tree here. No cypress, no pine, no oaks. But there was one thing that stood out to Raymond. One thing that let him know this was most certainly the spot he'd been last night.

On the ground, right around there where the tree had been, the underbrush, vegetation, and fallen leaves, were all blackened with decay. What's more, they floated and festered in a small black pool of water self contained in a perfect circle the size of the tree trunk had been.

Raymond stared, knowing that this circle of death made no sense at all. This isn't how things would decompose in nature. He rubbed his eyes until they hurt, hoping against hope that this was another vision that might be wiped away.

But he knew even as he did that, the vision wouldn't go away. He could still smell the rot.

TWELVE

TWO MONTHS LATER

Two months alone.

Raymond's deterioration never ceased. He never moved forward through the steps of grieving. Never found his way back toward healthy coping. Raymond knew this about himself on an intellectual level, yet made no moves to seek any real help or make any true changes.

At first he had been overwhelmed by the steady shipments of food sent to his door and the family and friends calling or just showing up out of the blue simply to check on him.

But eventually, the frozen food stocks ran out when the deliveries stopped. The calls grew further apart. Now, anytime someone did take the time to speak with him, they did so while uttering their words in soft, hushed tones and in carefully constructed, practiced sentences. Raymond considered this altered form of communication required far more effort than just having a straight conversation with a person. The people that populated the various social circles of his life were probably just of having to use the kid-gloves too. That kind of forced gentleness can grow exhausting. He asked himself:

Will they ever treat me like they used to...like normal?

He answered his question with another question:

Depends Raymond. When will you start acting normal?

He really had no idea what that even meant anymore.

It was his untold, unshared secret that marked his descent, his falling away from the Raymond his friends and family had known and had loved.

The figure.

The woman.

The one who announced her presence with a color, just a simple blue, just moments after Theresa's memorial service had concluded.

Who'd reminded him what that color had been at the reception.

Who'd began to haunt him to earnest, frozen like a matte painting behind the neighborhood houses as they streamed from peripheral to peripheral.

Who'd stood in the trees beyond the boundaries of his yard and watched. Beckoned. Gave him just enough to look upon to know that she was, in fact, a she. Then led him on a futile pursuit through those same trees, stopping at a point just far enough away from him where her outline, her shape, even that maddening blue color she projected had begun to blur in his range of vision.

His true point of entry into unbridled, all-consuming obsession began there.

Desperate to prove to himself that he was not going insane he began to search online for answers. The thought had occurred to him somewhere in the stretch of endless time that the last few weeks had been that maybe something was wrong with his eyes. Seeing one particular color dance on the sides of is vision is how it started. Maybe there was something to be found there. Raymond began researching, to the best of his ability, visual hallucinations that took place specifically in peripheral vision. He looked for visual hallucinations that took place only in one color.

He found information about retinal deterioration, eye disorders, and various illnessess. Many of these flirted with the things he had seen. None of them ever seemed to be a perfect fit. None of them were so personal, so realistic, or so haunting.

Every night after work, and some days during work, Raymond would search. Hours of time that consistently turned up nothing that truly fit. But still, Raymond searched.

Desperately searching for disorders of the peripheral vision. Desperately trying to not search for hauntings.

THIRTEEN

Almost out of pure desperation, Raymond weighed a return to working in office, instead of at home. He thought he'd be forcing himself out and away from that boundless yet self-contained void in which he'd spiraled for the past two months. He also considered that doing as such was a tangible, visible step towards "normal" for him. And if others knew he'd made the switch, all the better.

Yet he knew he wasn't even close to being ready to returning the office in person. Logging on to his company's intranet from home instead of onsite had become as much a curse as it had been, at least at first, a blessing.

When Theresa was alive it was wonderful. They both worked from home and both had their own little work spaces. They'd have their own coffee breaks, but they shared their lunchtimes together. And, there were no commutes for either of them to navigate -so when they were done they were done and they could get on with the rest of their day with not so much as a whiff of traffic-realted stress or frustration.

But now that Raymond was alone, the conveniences of working from home took on far different shapes within the context of his life without Theresa.

For example:

He'd never needed or had to dress himself for office life. He never saw, much less interacted with his colleagues outside of Zoom or Teams meetings. But while Theresa was still around, Raymond would still have to at least have to maintain personal hygiene, still get himself dressed in clothes he hadn't slept in the night before, still execute basic grooming rituals. Now that she was gone, the requirement to do any of these even if it was only for Theresa's sake, was gone.

This resulted in his wearing the same pair of pajamas for days on end. Showering became a once or twice per week event, and not first thing he did each day. His teeth had taken on distinctly yellowish tint.

And that was just for starters.

Raymond couldn't recall the last time he'd even left the house, save for his excursion into the woods the week before. That experience.

Today was going to be different though, through no choice of his own. The frozen food had finally run out, the bread had been finished with breakfast, no cereal left, not even a single can of soup. He needed to go grocery shopping. The very notion was incredibly daunting at this point, but he had little choice. If he had any capacity to plan ahead in these days, he might have been able to figure out the calculus of having his groceries delivered.

But the time for that had passed. It was likely for the best, all things considered.

So he warned his coworkers that he might be a little long on lunch and headed off to the grocery store. It would be the first time he actually did the shopping like this in… well years, actually. Theresa had always handled this chore. If had ever found himself at the grocery store, it was to grab milk and bread, or some other such immediate necessities. While she was sick, real sick at least, he normally just grabbed what he needed for a day or two and nothing more.

And she had always said she never minded shopping, whenever Raymond had expressed a half-hearted guilt about never performing this task nearly as much as she done over the years. Before Amanda moved out and particularly when she was little, grocery shopping was "a little break for mom." While Raymond didn't quite understand what that meant, he knew it at least meant she considered it to be an opportunity for alone time where she didn't have to be in mom or wife mode.

But today, Raymond certainly didn't feel like this would be a break of any sort for him. Quite the opposite, in fact. This was going to be a daunting experience but he was hoping that by going at noon on a Tuesday, the amount of people there would be considerably less.

Less people to avoid potentially having to make small talk, or even eye contact with.

Upon arriving at the closest FoodWorld, he found his assumption to be correct. The store parking lot was so empty that under any other circumstances, he would have assumed the location to be closed. A degree of relief washed over him.

Raymond parked and walked to the store. He grabbed a carriage on the way in. The automatic doors slid open and that cold, recycled grocery air washed over him. It calmed him. He then heard the inoffensive soft-rock soundtrack quietly playing in the background. He even recognized the song.

Goo Good Dolls... Iris he thought.

Strangely the anxiety that normally came with entering the grocery store never hit. Perhaps, after what he had recently been through, shit like picking out fruit and brand of cereal among strangers no longer passed the stress test? He wasn't sure the science or psychology behind it, but he also didn't care. He was just happy to be walking in here feeling like a normal person.

And for the first time in a while, he wasn't thinking about the tree. Not thinking about... her.

As he started down the first aisle he realized he hadn't actually made a list of things he needed. For the first time in what felt like forever, he chuckled. It was an absurd thing, being here without a list. But goddamn, it felt like such a normal, silly problem. It wasn't a dead wife. It wasn't figures in the distance. It was minutiae.

So he wandered up and down every aisle of the store, picking things up and dropping them in his basket as he remembered them and as they piqued his interest. He was probably out of many things at home that he didn't realize he was out of, but right now, it didn't matter much to Raymond. This had always been a trial run, right from the start. He would have some food to get him through and he would make a list next time – even if next time was just another day or two.

When he had made the trip down the last aisle, he figured he had found everything he was going to find, so he headed to checkout.

Raymond hated the very concept of self-checkout, so he made his way to the one register that had a person working behind it. He started piling his food on the conveyor, even making small talk with the cashier as she scanned his food.

The small talk eventually tapered off. Raymond's gaze wandered from watching his selections roll past on the conveyor towards the scanner to outside the store, though one of the huge series of windows that made up nearly the entire front face of the store.

He surveyed the parking lot. Then, past the parking to the the street. On the opposite side of the street, apartment complexes, up and down, .stretching beyond the range of his vision to both his left and right. His eyes came back around to where he had parked. Just outside the window he looked through, no more than thirty or forty feet from the entrance/exit doors of the store.

And standing next to his car was the figure.

No trees to hide behind. No paracentral regions in the outer range of his vision to disguise herself within. A person, a human, standing in a a prking lot devoid of any other individuals making their way to or from the store.

It was Theresa.

Of course it was Theresa.

Raymond Dolen mustered what remained of his willpower, his grip on reality, his sanity after the vast majority of each had simply drained from his body like toilet water at the mere sight of his wife. He did this to keep from doing one thing.

Seeing Theresa just standing there, watching him, it took everything in him not to scream.

FOURTEEN

Raymond slowly pushed his carriage away from him so he could step through the narrow checkout line. Pushing the rickety thing aside, he shambled, zombie-like up to the window. All the while, he never broke eye contact with Theresa, terribly afraid that she would disappear again again. Terribly afraid that she would stay.

She appeared exactly as she had just before she had gotten sick. Her black hair going down her back, longer and thicker too than most women. She had been letting it naturally go gray, but it took its time. It had given it a beautiful naturally streaked look.

"Who needs highlights, when I've got mother naure," she had joked.

He could make out the shine of the lip gloss she always wore. He could see the mascara around her deep blue eyes. He could see the curious look on her face, neither happy nor sad, purely inquisitive. He could see all this, despite her ethereal nature and faint blue glow..

The pink haired cashier looked up at him, confused and disturbed at the customer who broke the normal protocol of staying still and quiet during checkout. She looked around to find the manager in case things got weird. She cleared her throat.

"Uh that's 133.72." She half yelled at him, hoping to bring him back from the windows.

Raymond put his hands and forehead on the glass and stared at Theresa, mouth slightly agape. Her hair moved in the gentle breeze. She tilted her head to the side, as if asking a wordless question.

"Hey are you OK?" The cashier might as well have been talking to herself. "Did you hear me? You're all bagged up. ONE-THIRTY-THREE-SEVENTY-TWO"

Raymond followed the long windows along the front of the store trying to keep eye contact with Theresa. Before he got to the exit he was jogging, but had to wait on the automatic doors.

"Sir! Hey!"

Once the doors released him, just around a corner and… a stone pillar of the building cut off his view of Theresa for a split second.

She was gone.

Raymond ran frantically to his car. But Theresa was nowhere to be seen.

He pounded his fists into the roof of his car and screamed in the empty parking lot.

FIFTEEN

"What-the-fuck-what-the-fuck-what-the-fuck-" Raymond repeated over and over as he paced his kitchen.

He poured himself a cup of coffee with shaking hands. Reaching into the fridge he realized he still had no cream.

"-the-fuck-what-the-fuck-WHATTHEFUCK?!" He threw his coffee mug into the sink, breaking something by the sound of it, though he didn't bother checking.

No cream. The grocery store cashier and the man Raymond presumed was her manager had eventually come out into the parking lot while he had been screaming. They, of course, had not seen Theresa. They had been wondering why he abandoned his cart in line. But then they had looked concerned and scared.

"I... I'm sorry. Something's come up!" Raymond had yelled across the parking lot, before scrambling into his car and speeding out of the lot. He knew they thought he was crazy.

When Theresa got sick she had started smoking weed. Sometimes it helped with the pain, sometimes with the nerves or sadness. Raymond had joked with her about it being like it was back in high school. He rarely ever partook with her as adults, but certainly didn't disapprove. Anything that helped her in any way, emotional or physical, was fine by him. Right now, he just hoped she had some left.

He rummaged through her upstairs office until he found the drawer that she had kept her supplies in. The drawer was in a small wooden side table with a lamp and ash tray on the top. He found a lighter and a tube that contained three pre-rolled joints. There was more in the drawer, but the pre-rolls seemed the easiest bet at the moment.

He lit the joint and breathed in deeply. He tried to hold it in, but he almost instantly started coughing. It had been a while. He knew he didn't have to care about technique. He had a low tolerance and this was medical grade.

After another few drags he knew it was going to be more than enough. He snuffed the joint in the ash tray. He was fairly certain you weren't supposed to snuff joints that way, but it didn't matter that much right now.

He sat in Theresa's office chair as he felt the world slow down. His racing thoughts moved to a gallop, then a trot, and finally a comfortable canter. He couldn't make any more sense of what had happened, but at least he didn't feel like he was in a full blown panic.

Theresa's phone sat on the wireless charger on her desk. Amanda put it there when they brought her stuff home from the hospital after she died. He picked it up and swiped it open.

A picture of Theresa, Amanda, and he, had been set as her background. He recognized this one very clearly. It had been taken on father's day last year. Roughly a month before they got the news about Theresa's illness. Raymond always had mixed feeling about this picture. It was so sweet and so happy, but also felt so, naive, in way. It was like one of those photos that was in an internet compilation "Pictures Taken Moments Before a

Disaster."

He saw her Spotify app in the corner. He opened it. They had a playlist they used for almost everything. Driving. Parties. House cleaning. Whatever. He hadn't put it on since she'd passed. It was only on her phone. He hit the shuffle button. The algorithm chose Zepplin's "Fool in the Rain." He was slightly surprised when the music came from the speaker on the shelf over her desk instead of the phone. Her Bluetooth had automatically connected.

For a moment he let the music wash over him. In his slightly altered state he felt almost relaxed for the first time in months. He wasn't thinking about anything at all and just existing.

Eventually he got out of the seat and just started wandering the room. He looked around the office feeling surprisingly happy and comfortable in here. He had avoided this room for so long. Everything in here was just concentrated Theresa. But right now, in this moment, that was ok. It was nostalgic and good.

He saw her knickknacks, Disney figures, snow globes from all different places, a small and intricate little clock she had found while antiquing, so many pictures of her and Amanda and of him, her whole book collection that ranged from romance to horror, the current book left open on her desk, a compilation from Shirley Jackson currently opened to "The Lottery."

So many things. So uniquely her.

The playlist continued. "Tuesday's Gone"

He picked up everything he saw, observing it closely, before returning it to its previous and exact position. Sometimes he had to take in the details of the object and wonder exactly why she liked it enough to keep in here to see every day, other times, he knew almost instantly.

Spotify paused. The silence was immediate and jarring.

His cell phone rang. He pulled it out to see who it was.

A video call was being requested. From Theresa. From the phone that sat on the wireless charger. On the desk. In this room.

He stared at his phone. His finger hung over the answer button. But a dread rose up in him. He wanted to see Theresa of course, more than anything he ever remembered wanting. But like this? Was this even her? What would she be like, even if it was her? It could never be the same could it?

Raymond looked back up to Theresa's phone. Spotify minimized, the family picture that served as the background for Theresa's phone showing now. The picture started to blink, slowly at first, in and out of view, picture, then darkness. Faster, and faster it went, until it strobed like the vision of the figure, of Theresa, behind the houses and behind the ceiling fan

A fear grew in him. It was visceral. Instinctual. Fear of the grave. Whatever this was and wherever it was from, it was from a place that was supposed to be unknown and supposed to stay unknown.

He started furiously trying to deny the call. No matter how many times he hit that red button it would no drop it. The ringing got louder. It was coming from the bluetooth speaker now too. The volume rising. His stupid innocuous ring tone blaring at an ear-shattering volume, insisting he answer this call.

Instead he ran from the room and slammed the office door.

His phone stopped ringing.

"Running to the Edge of the World" began playing on Spotify, as if it had simply moved to the next track.

Raymond went downstairs.

SIXTEEN

"Dad... maybe its time you talked to somebody, huh?"
Raymond adjusted the cordless landline phone in its position between his shoulder and ear. He sat at the bar height section of his kitchen counter. Tears rolled down his face silently, without sobs or resistance, steadily leaking, like a garden hose with a nozzle in need of tightening left on a driveway forging small paths over the dirty asphalt of his face.

"Mandy..." A pause. Amanda heard what she knew to be ice tapping against the sides of a bourbon glass as her father took a sip. "...honey I am trying to talk to *you.*"

"You know what I mean. A professional."

"Oh Amanda, come on..."

"Dismissive. Again." Amanda sighed, trying to steady herself. *Be firm, not mean.* "My ideas are valid. I am a grown adult and sometimes its possible I could actually have good advice."

"But a *psychiatrist?*" He spat the last word out like it was sour.

"Dad. Stop. Please. Mom is gone but you think you are seeing her everywhere? She's calling you on the phone? This isn't normal. You're chasing ghosts. Please-"

Raymond hung up the phone. He should have known how he would sound. Like a raving madman. Indeed. It didn't mean he wanted everybody he talked to telling him to go see a goddamn shrink.

Maybe she was right though. He was scared. One way or another, he was chasing ghosts, in his mind, or in the world.

Spotify continued to play in the office upstairs.

"Dancing With Myself"

SEVENTEEN

Amanda sat on her couch, rubbing her temples. Not for the first time, she looked at her phone that lay discarded on the coffee table and thought about calling her father back. But in this mood he was in, it was unlikely she would get any further with the conversation she was trying to have or the point she was trying to make. That's assuming he even answered the phone, which she had a feeling he would not do.

She'd pushed too hard, apparently. That thought in and of itself, started to piss her off. No, she hadn't pushed to hard. Its that she had the apparent audacity to suggest that he talk to somebody. Apparently, according to him and so many of his generation, "talking to someone" was reserved only for those already locked away in the nut house. Lunatics, hysterics, spazzes, idiots, and whatever other antiquated slanders directed against those with "real" mental health issues. So many people his age had had it beaten into them that they just needed to suck it up, deal with it, or get thicker skin, because so many people were worse off than they were. But there were no heroics or bravery in suppressing your emotions like this. They would come out some other way. They always did.

Moreover, he used the word "psychologist," not her. A psychologist would have been fine, a therapist, a grief councilor. Anybody with proper certifications and training. This was getting out of hand. Some of the things he was saying and seeming to believe were starting to get worrisome. Disturbing really. Amanda could feel herself losing control of the situation.

Maybe the situation isn't yours to control. She heard the words of her own therapist in her head. And maybe it wasn't. But if it is slipping out of Dad's control and it isn't mine to control, then what will happen?

She could feel the anger and annoyance at her father's stubbornness start to give way as it was overrun by the old familiar feelings of anxiety. The fluttering in her chest. Breathing that was starting to speed up. Those extra jolts of fight or flight energy shooting into her arms and legs, with nowhere to go. Her knee started bouncing in place. She almost started biting her nails like she did when she was young, but caught herself - there was polish on them and she didn't want to eat that or ruin how they looked. With nothing left to do, her hands started clenching and unclenching, leaving deep indents in her palms, from those polished nails.

She leaned back on the couch, trying to begin the breathing techniques her therapist showed her. But as the air shuddered its way into her lungs, she knew it wasn't going to work. This was going to be a full blown anxiety attack. She would have to ride it out or dip into the "only for emergencies" Xanax she'd been prescribed.

When it came down to it, if a newly dead mom and a dad that very well may be coming unraveled is not what one considered "an emergency" than nearly nothing would be.

What if that is just the panic speaking? Are you over reacting? Are

55

you going to take a Xanax every little time you get a case of nerves?

She had had anxiety long enough to know that when her thoughts were going this fast, she was far gone. The rationality that was still there in her brain, that was fighting to be heard over all this noise, told her she wasn't over reacting and that it had been months since she'd even considered the Xanax. The therapy was working, she just needed some help this time.

She went into the kitchen in search of the medication. Her body giving slight tremors and her head reverberating with panic. She kept her antidepressants next to her coffee mugs. She kept them there so she wouldn't forget to take them. Behind them sat the Xanax, nearly untouched.

"Alprazolam. Take ½ pill (.5mg) as needed for anxiety. No automatic refills."

She threw back the Xanax, drinking half her bottle of water in the process. She sat there, on her kitchen floor, with her back against the cabinet, knees to her chest and cried into her jeans.

After what could have been minutes or could have been hours the anxiety finally began to ebb. The calm starts with the adrenaline that was trying to escape from her hands and legs giving up on its struggle, admitting defeat and crawling back quietly into the recesses of her mind. Her thoughts begin to slow and she is suddenly able to concentrate on her breathing techniques. Her heart stops fluttering, and finally remembers its normal pattern and falls back into rhythm. It was over.

Amanda let her knees slide away from her chest and extend, her legs going out straight in front of her. Her head fell back to lean against the cabinets. She let her head loll to the side so she could glance at the clock. It was just after five.

She dragged herself to her feet and over to the fridge. She pulled a frozen dinner from the freezer and tossed it in the microwave. Watching it spin, she thought about why she was like this. Why she had to have this anxiety. She always had this kind of contemplation, post attack. The self reflection of somebody who wished they could just be normal.

She thought back to when she was young. All those plans her parents made. All that time they were so desperately in love with each other. All those times she was such an after thought. So many of those vacations all over the world they went on while she stayed with Aunt Tina.

They loved her. Especially Dad. But Dad would just kind of go along with whatever Mom wanted to do and however she wanted to do it. He was in love and never wanted to upset her. Mom loved her too, but in that way that one does when they are "supposed to." She wanted to keep up the appearance of the perfect little family. She wanted it ideal. She wanted the smiling family pictures. Sometimes she felt like Mom loved the idea of a daughter rather than her actual daughter.

When they were off on those trips without her, that's when this all really started. Amanda, probably being starved for actual affection from her mother, started to become concerned, anxious, even arguably paranoid about bad things happening to them while they were gone. She worried the cruise ship would sink, that the plane would crash, that they would be kidnapped or killed or otherwise never seen again. Poor Aunt Tina had a lot of late nights trying to calm her down.

The microwave beeped. She pulled out the dinner and tossed it on the kitchen table. She decided to wash it down with a glass of wine, knowing full well that her night would be over and done with by 6:30. The alcohol mixing with the Xanax and beckoning her to a sleep that would be deep and dreamless and drag her through into tomorrow.

EIGHTEEN

He was having the dream again. It was the last time Raymond had seen Theresa alive. Although, at this point, alive was a technicality.

As always, Raymond sat with Theresa in the hospital room. And as always she was a thin reflection of her former self. Her hair, like always, was gone, covered up by the bandanna with the boxing kittens. Every time he saw this now, it was even more sad and ironic than the last.

She'd only been awake for a short time that day, maybe a half hour. She wasn't really able to speak anymore. But they had looked at each other lovingly, wordlessly, until she started to drift to sleep again and Raymond told her he loved her. A hint of a smile had crossed her face, she mouthed "I love you" and she'd closed her eyes.

Something burned in the back of Raymond's brain, even asleep. She had never moved her mouth that day. This wasn't right.

The dream continued, undeterred by his unease.

He stayed with her until after the worst of the traffic had subsided in the city surrounding the hospital. Finally he gave his sleeping wife one last squeeze of her hand and a kiss on her forehead. He felt her squeeze his hand in return.

Wrong! She never -

He walked to the doorway of the room, looking back on her in the bed. The machines around her quietly beeped, hummed, and exhaled. Cards and flowers decorated the window behind her. A whiteboard on the wall announced the name of the nurse on duty "Tiffany."

Where is the... ?

"Goodbye, my love"

NINETEEN

It was two days before Raymond worked up the courage to go back into Theresa's office and shut off Spotify. Their playlist was 10 hours long and set to repeat. It had persisted those two days, and would have continued to, presumably forever with the phone sitting on the charger.

He picked the phone up and paused the music. He force-closed Spotify and though it pained him, he shut Theresa's phone off and placed it in the top drawer of her desk. He pushed the drawer shut.

And as simple as that, all the sound was gone. The quiet hung heavy after days of music. The silence carried with it a shroud of loss, that it draped over the whole house. As this reticent pall was draped, he felt like he couldn't breathe. The silence felt air tight.

He tried to speak but no words came out. He tried to cough, but there was only silence. The breath he tried to drawn in carried no oxygen, only silence. He began to panic, his clothes made no shuffling sounds, and his hands slapping at his throat made no noise at all.

His bulging eyes landed on the antique clock. He watched the second hand jump forward a tick, then backward a tick, this moment dragging into eternity.

Desperate, he grabbed the nearest thing he could reach and threw it at the wall.

The snow globe shattered, glass resonating and breaking the silence. He felt the sounds return to the world and his breath to him. The second hand of the clock resumed its forward pace.

His relief was short lived, once he saw what he'd done. The snow globe he'd thrown was the first one Theresa had bought. She got it on their honeymoon in Florida. They couldn't afford much of a honeymoon back then, but a Florida beach trip had seemed so wonderful. She wanted to commemorate the occasion by purchasing this silly little snow globe with some palm trees and flamingos inside and Miami Beach, FL written in colorful letters on the front. This one snow globe had started a tradition for her of getting a new one every time they'd gone on vacation.

Now, the glass lay scattered across the floor, the palm trees had snapped, and the flamingos were just… gone.

He collapsed on the floor, a broken pile, just as much as the snow globe beside him. He'd given away a part of Theresa, trying to save himself. He could never get it back. He cried, knowing that pieces could just slip away and never return. Time would take it all.

TWENTY

The next day, Raymond dragged himself from bed, exhausted. His eyes were puffy and dark, old yellowing cases hiding lumpy deflated pillows. His temples throbbed and his neck ached.

He walked to the bathroom and washed his face, using the coldest water he could stand. He dropped the towel and looked into the mirror. He used his hands to brush the hair from his face and straight back over his head. The gray that used to only appear on his temples had somehow snuck strands into the rest of his hair, here and there. The term "salt and pepper" crossed his mind, even though his hair was brown. But watching as his hair slowly showed more white, Raymond couldn't help but think of a log that has been in a fire for ages, go past black and into white ash.

You're an old man. Raymond thought, despite it not being true. Sure, his daughter was grown and sure, he was deep into what one would call middle-aged, but he wasn't even of retirement age yet. But with the grays and the bags under his eyes, he felt like he was pushing one hundred.

He had felt displaced in time for a while now. Even before Theresa died. Even before she was diagnosed. His own father had died at forty. Since his forty-first birthday Raymond had felt like he was on some kind of borrowed time. Maybe it was due to a latent survivor's guilt; not because he was supposed to die with his father, but simply because Raymond was older now than he had ever seen his own father. He'd known his grandfather and that man had lived into his early nineties, stubborn angry goat that he was, but he had always been "old" in Raymond's perspective. Raymond existed in the middle now.

No man's land.

The thought crossed his mind that maybe Amanda would feel like that someday, with her mom gone. But he hoped, since she was already an adult, it wouldn't hit her as hard.

Raymond wiped a dry towel across his face, hoping it would take these thoughts with it.

He went downstairs and made his way to the kitchen, opening the blinds and shades of the windows as he went, if for nothing more than out of simple habit. He pressed the button to start the coffee pot's heating process while he took out a the expended single cup pod from yesterday, placing it on a saucer on his counter. He took out a new pod and put it in the coffee maker.

The familiar sound and smell of fresh pouring coffee filled the kitchen. He couldn't help but think how this used to always be the first of two he used to make at once. One for himself and one for Theresa. His with the regular cream and sugar, hers with no sugar, but that hazelnut flavored creamer.

Raymond looked in the fridge and realized that old creamer was still there. It was non-dairy, so it was likely just fine, but nobody else liked it. He and Amanda both took their coffee unflavored. He took the creamer from the fridge and examined it for a bit, lost in his own thoughts and memories.

The coffee maker made the tell tale sputtering sound of a coffee that was done being poured. Raymond looked from the creamer to his coffee cup. Eventually, he sighed and brought it over to the sink, uncapped it and began to pour it out. He watched it circle and make its way to the drain.

He thought about the last few days. He was tired and scared. The conversation with Amanda had worried him most of all. He was sure, so sure, that he was seeing Theresa. So sure, that none of this was his imagination. But she didn't believe him.

Would Raymond have believed this story if somebody else told it to him? Probably not. But sometimes unbelievable things were quite real.

The last of the creamer disappeared down the drain.

TWENTY-ONE

He was having the dream again. It was the last time Raymond had seen Theresa alive. Again.

He was there with Theresa in the hospital room. She was more emaciated than he ever remembered seeing her. The bandanna wrapped around her bald scalp was covered in aggressively snarling bears, all teeth and anger and drool.

No, that's what they were fighting, right? Why...?

She'd only been awake for a short time that day, maybe a half hour. She wasn't really able to speak anymore. But they had looked at each other lovingly, wordlessly, until she started to drift to sleep again. Her mouth hung open and he could hear her breathe. The smell coming from the cavern of her mouth was of decay. Raymond gagged, even in the dream and stood up.

Wait! I was supposed to tell her I love her.

He stood next to the bed, no longer close to her face. He couldn't be near that rancid smell. He couldn't believe he was thinking of her like this either.

He stood like that as time went by, knowing he was there until the traffic eased up in the city. As the clock marched forward the flowers behind her bed rapidly aged, wilted, and blackened. The get well cards, yellowed and slowly fell apart. When all the

65

rotting was complete, he knew it must be time to go.

He walked to the doorway of the room and looked over at the white board. This time it said "Tiffany: I'll be calling you at 11:38 tonight to tell you she died. That you missed it."

He looked to Theresa's bed, preparing to say goodbye. But instead she was sitting up. Where seconds ago she was drooling, breath pure miasma, she was now sitting, looking as healthy as she ever did. He hair was back, she was a healthy weight.

This has definitely never happened before.

"Theresa? Hun? Is that…?" the words caught in his throat.

She didn't smile. Didn't react like he thought she would. She just looked at him and tilted her head to the side like she did, every time he had seen her recently.

In his mind he heard her say, "Will you stay with me, Ray? Can you?"

Can I? I don't know this rules. This is the part where I am supposed to leave.

The moment the thought of leaving crossed his mind, Theresa seemed to lose all the strength in he body. She fell back in the bed, and as she landed her appearance instantly changed. She looked, right down to the goddamn dress he had picked out, exactly as she did at her wake.

The hospital bed's protective sides popped up, but they were no longer the gray support bars, but the mahogany sides of a casket. The bed shrank and contracted. A lid appeared from nowhere, slamming shut. The bed-turned-coffin, retracted into the hospital floor, leaving Raymond standing in an empty hospital room alone.

He heard his own voice, distorted, raw, and dripping with venom, screaming in his ears. "GOOOODBYE, MYYYYY LOOOOOOVE!"

TWENTY-TWO

I t was three more days before he saw Theresa again. Three days of painful, empty, peace. Time filled with single cups of coffee, meals for one, and only his preferred TV shows. Vacant.

He sat on his porch at sunset. The days were starting to slowly stretch themselves longer and much of the chill was starting to slip from the air. He sat with his rocks glass, half-full with the last of the Woodford Reserve. He stared out into the woods. As the sun dipped far enough to be fully hidden by the trees, he saw her.

There she was, standing in the woods again. For a moment he just watched as she stood, motionless, pale and blue. He squinted trying to get a better view. It was hard to see because she was so far away.

That thought collided with him and knocked the wind out of him as surely as a boxing glove to the sternum. She was further away. Every time he'd seen her before she'd been coming closer. Last time he'd seen her she'd been so close he could see her lip gloss He'd see her and go after her and she'd be closer and now...

He'd ignored the phone call. He smashed the snow globe.

Now she was further away.

He jumped out of his seat trying to never break line of sight with her and ran. He ran like he hadn't since he was on the high school baseball team. He put everything into running. She was going to slip away.

He got to the edge of the woods and she had moved exactly as far into the woods. She wasn't walking as she moved away, but sliding straight away, as a magnet would when you bring one of the same pole too close. Part of him knew he wouldn't catch up. But he couldn't stop. As scared as he had been of the phone, it was nothing compared to this. Now he knew, if he didn't actively pursue her, she would drift further and further from him until she was gone from even his peripherals. He couldn't let that happen.

Far into the woods he was slowing, huffing. High school was a long ways back and he felt every year weighing on his chest. He kept trying to move, kept trying to follow. When suddenly, her head tilted to the side again, as if she was just now seeing him. Her feet planted on the ground and she stepped to the side, behind a tree.

And just like that, she was gone again.

Alone in the woods he wailed. He was tired through and through. From running. From crying. From existing.

Darkness had fully settled and he realized he could not see his house at all. He'd come a lot further into the woods than he'd thought and now he was good and turned around.

All he could do at this point was walk and hope it was the right direction. His cell phone had no reception but he could use the flashlight at least. He knew these woods well enough and knew they were relatively small, as far as woods went. And while he couldn't recognize much in the darkness, he figured he would eventually come to one of the edges and figure out a way home from there, whether it was his backyard or the other side of town.

He walked in the dark for what couldn't have been less than an hour and a half when he saw light coming through the trees. Feeling some sense of relief, he pushed on.

As he came out of the brush he knew he wasn't in a neighborhood anymore but somewhere downtown. It wasn't a big town by any means, but this area was clearly more commercial. He looked more closely at the building in front of him.

He didn't recognize it at first because he had come out behind the building in the back parking lot but after a moment he knew exactly what he was looking at.

The town's one screen movie theater. The movie theater he used to work at in his younger days. The movie theater where he'd met Theresa.

Cell reception was back. Happy that Amanda had convinced him to set him up Uber, he took out his phone and requested a pickup. Seconds after he finished requesting the ride, his phone started vibrating with alerts that it had missed when he had no service in the woods.

Missed call from Amanda.

Facebook nonsense.

10 new text messages. All of them empty. All of them from Theresa's phone.

He sat on the steps of the movie theater, laughing and crying all at once.

She was close again. He wouldn't lose her.

He's steadied himself enough by the time the Uber came to get him. He made small talk with the driver as she took him on the short trip back around town. She dropped him at his house, he thanked her and used the app to tip her before she even left his driveway.

He walked around the back of his house in the dark. The motion sensor turned on when he got to the porch. His whiskey was right where he'd left it. Glancing quickly to make sure no bugs had found their way in, he downed the glass in one gulp, smiling at the burn.

He went back into the house and deposited the empty glass in the sink. Not bothering with the TV or anything else that night, he made his way up to bed. Raymond slept well for perhaps the first time since Theresa had been diagnosed.

TWENTY-THREE

H is confidence was well placed, it seemed. The next day he saw her again. Theresa was just as close as she had been when he'd seen her from the grocery store. This time he'd seen her while he was driving.

He'd gone to Central Square Hardware to get some superglue and model paint. He was going to do what he could to at least fix the appearance of that snow globe. Even if it wasn't ever going to be functional again, at least he could put it back and display it. A few touch ups and some glue and it wouldn't look terrible.

He'd found his supplies in the store with relative ease. This was a smaller town and Raymond did what he could to shop locally, rather than going to the larger chain stores, which meant he was quite familiar with Central Square hardware. In turn, they were quite familiar with him.

He brought his purchases to the counter.

"Hey-a, Ray…" John said.

John was the owner of small hardware store. He looked at Raymond over the rims the small glasses he wore low on his nose. A note of concern crossed the old man's voice, a look somewhere between confusion and distaste on his face. Raymond ignored this.

"Hi John!" he said, sounding more excited than he expected himself too.

This contrast seemed to disarm the old man a bit. They made small talk as John rang him up.

As Raymond gathered his things to go, John asked, "Ray.. How you doing? Really?"

Raymond gave a half smile. "I'm gonna be OK, John. Really."

The men gave each other nods in place of goodbyes, and Raymond left the store. He got in the car, putting his things on the passenger seat. He started the car and the radio played, "Can't You See" as he pulled away from his spot next to the curb.

As he drove home from the small shop, he had to pass a town park. He glanced over, and there she was, clear as day, sitting on the bench, watching the passing cars.

He swerved suddenly into the makeshift dirt lot, causing some frustrated honking from the car behind him, but he didn't take his eyes off Theresa for a second. But as soon as he'd gotten himself out of the car, he realized his folly. In order to get to the bench from here, he would have to walk around the little league dugout. A high fence blocked the direct route. There was no way to go where he wouldn't lose sight of her, if even for an instant.

He knew he had to go over there. And he would. But for the moment he stood and he watched this spectral form of his wife from off to the side, while she watched the traffic. Her black hair hung over the back of the bench. He traced the profile of her face with his fingers, in his mind.

He took a deep breath and started walking. As he came to where the dugout would cut off his view he sped his pace, but he knew it wouldn't matter. And it didn't. When he saw the bench again, it was empty.

72

Raymond walked over to the bench anyway and sat down in the spot next to where Theresa had sat.

He could smell her scent lingering in the air. He held back the tears as he wouldn't risk his nose getting stuffy. He couldn't miss a second of this. Her shampoo. Her body wash. Her.

The wind blew and the scent was gone.

TWENTY-FOUR

"Honey, no. I was having a bad couple days the last time we talked. Its fine. It is. We all have different ways of dealing with things. I'm not afriad anymore. Its OK."

"I donno, Dad. You seemed pretty disconnected with reality last time…" Amanda said, real concern resonating in her voice.

"Mandy. I'm sorry. I must have scared you. I can't imagine any of that was easy to hear."

"It wasn't…"

"I've found some things to occupy my time. Some crafts. Things around the house. I do much better when I stay busy." Raymond tried to assure her.

"Ok." It was obvious that she wasn't fully convinced. "But I am going to keep checking in on you for the next few days. Try not to get too tired of these calls… I love you."

"I love you too, kid." He hung up the phone and went back to gluing the palm trees back to their original positions.

He had spent his work day working in Theresa's office instead of his own. He continued his crafted repairs of the snow globe in there as well. By the time he had finished his meticulous painting and repairs, the day had grown late. He placed the snow globe on the shelf, right where it had been and headed downstairs to make dinner.

He had found that all the work he had put into the repairs both kept his mind busy and allowed him a chance to reflect on happy times with her. The busyness allowed these thoughts to flow without crushing them in their weight, as they normally did.

Downstairs he put a pot on the stove and dumped a jar of pasta sauce in. He got a bigger pot, filled it with water and set it to boil. This was the first thing he'd made that more complex than a sandwich since Theresa died.

When the pasta had cooked and the sauce had heated he went and sat at the table like he and Theresa used to do. All this time since she'd been in the hospital, he'd eaten at the counter, on the couch, or even over the sink. But tonight Raymond sat there in his usual seat, across from her usual seat and ate a proper meal like an adult.

When he'd finished, he cleared the table, got what he could in the dishwasher and turned it on right then. A full meal and cleanup had taken place like it always used to, back when things were right. This simple set of tasks hand brought an incredible sense of normalcy.

Raymond sat on the couch and found something on television that was at least a little mentally engaging. It was some older show that a detective figuring out mysteries week to week. He followed along and made his guesses, some right, most wrong. Regardless of his accuracy, it was still more stimulating than the sitcoms that no longer made him laugh. After about three hours of television, he went upstairs to ready himself for bed.

Raymond showered and put on a thin t-shirt and some pajama bottoms. He brushed his teeth and went back to his room. He ran his hand across Theresa's dresser and looked into the attached mirror. He almost looked like himself again, after

75

weeks of looking exhausted and disheveled.

Raymond laid down on his side of the bed and felt relaxed. He could almost feel her there with him. After all this time he felt almost normal. The realization that he felt even a little good brought tears of guilt to his eyes. Even so, he was quickly and blissfully asleep.

TWENTY-FIVE

Raymond felt himself falling and woke with a start. He looked around and realized it was still the middle of the night and he must have been dreaming, though strangely, this time he remembered nothing. As he was about to close his eyes and go back to sleep, he realized the motion sensor light in the back yard had turned on.

He went to the window and looked down into the yard. There was nothing in the circle of light provided by the sensor's spotlight right now, but he had a feeling he knew what was out there.

He went to Theresa's office and grabbed the Bluetooth speaker and her phone from the drawer, turning them both on as he walked. He came down the stairs and headed out of the side door of his house.

Once outside he gently picked some flowers from flowerbed near the door and walked toward the back of the house. There he paused and held his breath. He waited and after what seemed like forever, the motion sensor shut off.

And there she was. Theresa. No more than twenty feet away, now visible, showing right where the light had been shining. Tears filled Raymond's eyes, when she smiled at him and extended her hands towards him.

Despite all the movement, the motion sensor light never came back on. But he didn't need it, Theresa, in this full darkness of the night, glowed ever so slightly. She was beautiful.

He turned on Spotify as he slowly walked to her. He hit shuffle on their playlist and so very appropriately, "Unchained Melody" began. He place the speaker and her phone in the grass and went to her.

This time she didn't move away. She didn't duck behind anything. She stayed. He reached out, handing her the flowers, which she took from him before throwing her arms around the back of his neck and embracing him. They pulled each other close and kissed deeply.

The world around them seemed to disappear as they slowly danced in the yard to their favorite songs. It was just them and Raymond could swear she looked just like she did on that first trip to Miami, all those years ago. He felt as alive as he did back then too, here in the arms of his wife, who he'd thought he'd lost forever.

TWENTY-SIX

A manda Dolen had not heard from her father in three days. And not for lack of trying. At this point, they were still talking in some capacity every day. Over the last three days she had called, texted, and even emailed but had received no response at all.

The anxiety she always seemed to be filled with had come to a boiling point and she couldn't stand it anymore. Her concern for her father growing too great, she went to her car. As she pulled from the lot of her apartment and into the midday traffic, her phone connected to her car stereo and music flooded the car. "Best Day of My Life." Before the little guitar diddy at the beginning had even finished, her anxiety was pushed even further, making her shake. She slammed her hand into the controls, shutting the music off.

She drove, in silence, trying desperately to implement the breathing techniques her therapist had taught her.

When she first made it to her father's house, nothing seemed out of place. She saw his car in the driveway, right where it always was. But as she parked behind him and got out of the car a sense of dread rose in her. Her anxiety was always quick and jittery. This dread rose in her slow and plodding. It was patient and heavy.

As she walked from the driveway to the side door, she saw that the flowers from the middle of the flowerbed by the door had been ripped out, all the way down to the roots. There was dirt all over the place making it difficult to tell what had happened or which direction they might have been carried off in.

Furrowing her brow she went to the door and was about to knock, but it just pushed open, having never been properly shut in the first place. She walked into her old childhood home, feeling like it was a foreign land.

"Dad?" she called out. No response.

Despite the midday sun outside, it was dark in here. Her dad had never opened all the shades and blinds this morning. She opened them as she moved through the house, as much to be able to see properly, as it was to complete this simple morning ritual her dad normally took care of every day.

After opening the blinds in the kitchen, she looked around. The unwashed dishwasher hung open. This sink was filled with dirty dishes and broken glass. Coffee pods littered the counter and floors near the coffee maker. There was a mostly empty and severely burned pot of pasta sauce on the stove. She looked at the kitchen table and grimaced.

There was a plate of pasta on the table in what used to be her mom's spot. It looked like it had been sitting there for days. The chair remained pushed all the way in on that side, though her father's side was pulled out still as if somebody had just stood up.

A fly buzzed past her ear breaking her out of these contemplations. She waved it off and shook her head. She watched as it flew back to the counter to hover around mug after mug, filled with old coffee and lightened with hazelnut creamer. She could smell it, sick and sweet, even from where she stood. She was starting to feel nauseous.

She went back to opening the shades and looking through the first floor of the house, but nothing more was out of place. She made her way upstairs.

Coming onto the upstairs landing she noticed her mom's office door was open. She hesitated. The last time she was in this room she was bringing mom's phone back from the hospital after she died. She knew she had to check all the rooms in the house though.

"Dad are you-?" she trailed off as she entered the room. The wall across from the door had a large hole in the drywall with some kind of water stain around it.

What the fuck?

Trying to give any kind of context to this she looked around the room. One of the desk drawers was flung open, some papers now sticking out everywhere. Mom's bluetooth speaker that Amanda had got for her was missing from it's usual perch, the power cord hanging from the shelf. Then she saw the snow globe.

Sitting on the end of the shelf was one of mom's famous snow globes. Or what was left of it. It was pretty safe to say that this is what had made the dent in the wall. The glass orb had been shattered and the decorative pieces inside broken. It looked as if dad had tried to reassemble it somehow, but it was all so wrong.

The trees were glued but not to their stumps, just haphazardly. The flamingo's neck was at a horrid angle. Worst of all the glass in the globe had been glued back in a way that only made it a jagged and horrible half circle. Judging by what looked like blood on the glass, he had put that together first and cut up his hands trying to do the rest of this assembly.

Jesus, Dad. Ouch...

Amanda left the office and headed to her parent's bedroom. It was somehow even more of a mess than the office had been. Her mom's dresser drawers were all opened. Clothes were strewn everywhere. The mirror was cracked, looking as if it had been punched. Fluttering curtains let her know that the window that faced the back yard was wide open. The ceiling fan was on, turned up to its highest setting and shaking slightly, as if the bolts holding it in its perch were beginning to give way.

She shut the ceiling fan off and made her way further into the bedroom.

Amanda saw the TV was on then. It was on that old re-run channel that had the shows the adults watched when she was a kid. She hadn't noticed the TV was on before walking in because there was no sound. The soundbar that was normally hanging under the TV seemed to be missing.

She looked down at the bed. The covers were pulled up and there was a human sized lump underneath. She steadied herself, thinking she was about to find her father, and pulled the covers back revealing three pillows. It dawned on her that these were on Mom's side.

Dad must have lined these up like this so he didn't feel alone in the bed...

She was about to cover the pillows back up when she realized one more thing about them. Each of them, between the pillow and pillow case, had been stuffed full with her mom's clothes.

Oh God that's weird. Why would you... did they smell like her... Oh Dad...

She covered them back up and went over to shut the window. She wanted nothing more than to get out of here now. She quickly finished checking the house and, finding nothing more, got herself outside.

She leaned against the side of the house, tears in her eyes. She stayed there for a moment, letting the tears finish themselves, having grown all too used to this process lately. She wiped what was left from her eyes and pushed her hair out of her face and in doing so noticed something out of place in the back yard.

She sighed, not even sure she wanted to know, but pushing herself forward. She looked down at the objects sitting in the grass. Mom's phone and Bluetooth speaker, both completely drained of battery. As she picked them up she noticed something reflective by the house.

The grass in that area was covered in white glass. It took her a moment to process, but she eventually looked up. The outside motion sensor light had been shattered. Shards stuck out of the socket still. It seemed like somebody must have thrown a rock at it.

TWENTY-SEVEN

Having finished searching the house she went back and sat in her car. She leaned her head back on the seat and stared at the ceiling. At this point she could only assume her dad had had some kind of episode and wandered off. She had to look for him.

Part of her thought she should call the police. But she wasn't ready to accept that yet. She had to try for herself first. Maybe there was some kind of reasonable explanation still, though her mind struggled to put together anything that made sense.

She drove around town going any place she could think of that he liked. She checked the local doughnut shop where he went for breakfast on occasion. She went by the grocery store. Not seeing any signs of him at either of these places, she moved on.

She went to the little hardware store he loved so much. She went inside knowing that they knew him by name. Maybe they'd seen him. When she walked in, the man she recognized as the owner stood from his seat at the counter.

"Oh, hello there, Amanda," he said. Despite her panic, she still felt a pang of guilt in her gut for not remembering the old man's name.

"Hi. I'm sorry. I don't mean to be short but I am looking for my father. I haven't heard from him in days. Have you seen him?"

"Last I saw him... Tuesday? Wednesday?" he said, scratching at some stubble.

"Shit. OK. Thank you." Amanda said, making for the door.

"Kid?" He said, with a sudden urgency. When she stopped and turned he added, "He didn't look good. Thousand yard stare, even when he was looking right at me. Think he was still in pajamas..." The old man trailed off not sure what else to add.

Amanda closed her eyes for a moment, trying to get her bearings. She sighed.

"Thank you," she said, and made for the door before the tears could form in her eyes.

She drove up and down through the center of town, hoping to catch him walking. She was starting to lose hope of finding him and was about to call the police, but slowed as she drove by the cemetery.

She pulled her car in and drove toward that secluded spot she and her dad had picked out those few weeks prior. She parked her car where the thin road came to an end and got out, not even taking the time to shut the door. She walked up the hill and to the tree, under which, her mother's grave stood.

There she found her father. He was laying on the ground on him stomach, with his head to the side. He laid as if he were hugging the ground in front of the grave with a look on his face as peaceful as Amanda had ever seen him wear. He was in his pajamas, his bare feet filthy. He clutched the flowers in his hand that he'd ripped from beside the house. He was dead.

Back in the car, out of Amanda's earshot, the Bluetooth speaker shot to life just long enough the play the last verse of "Moon Over Miami" before the battery ran out for good.

EPILOGUE

Amanda terminated the call. The police were on their way and would figure out what to do with her father's body.

Tears filled her eyes and blurred her vision. She blinked, they fell. The world came back into focus.

She cried the tears of an unavoidable event coming to pass, more than a sudden tragedy. Deep down, she knew, whether she could admit it to herself or not, that her father would not make it in the world without her mother. She always knew.

He followed her wherever she went. Even into death.

Tears filled her eyes and blurred her vision. She blinked, they fell. The world came back into focus.

She wondered what this meant for her. Her childhood was shaped by what they wanted to do and had planned for themselves. Such a chunk of her adult life had been focused around helping where she could after her mother got sick. And the last few months she had tried in vein to help her father keep his life together. Now it was just her. Alone. She had few friends and mediocre job. What was her life now when it was just her? Alone.

Tears filled her eyes and blurred her vision. She blinked, they fell. The world came back into focus, save for the two fluttering, pale, blue lights, dancing in the edges of her vision.

Printed in the USA
CPSIA information can be obtained
at www.ICGtesting.com
LVHW010925101123
763485LV00091B/3879